This Little Tiger book
belongs to:

_____

_____

_____

IT'S TIME TO SLEEP, YOU CRAZY SHEEP!

Alison Ritchie   illustrated by Cornelia Haas

LITTLE TIGER PRESS
London

Tucked up tight, all warm and snug,
Phoebe tries to sleep.
She shuts her eyes, but she's not tired:
she needs to count her sheep!

But Phoebe's sheep have other plans –
they're bored of jumping gates.
They're heading for the ice rink,
and putting on their skates.

Now they're revving up their bikes.
They like to travel fast!

"Wait!" cries Phoebe, but her sheep just wave as they whizz past.

They've reached the highest cliff top now.
"Come **back** here!" Phoebe begs.
But off they fly into the sky,

ballet,
woolly ewes
whirl and dance
ballet shoes.

"Stop it, stop it!" Phoebe wails.

"Let me count you, please!"

But her sheep zoom down the slope,

Zig-zagging through the trees.

BOING!

Bouncing on a trampoline,
up and down they go.
Like daring circus acrobats,
they're putting on a show!

Off they go to football,
to dribble, duck and dive.
Another goal! The whistle blows:
the home team wins six-five.

"Stop!" shouts Phoebe. "Stop it now!
I'm still wide awake!"
But Phoebe's sheep are boiling hot,
and flocking to the lake.

With double flips and somersaults,
into the lake they leap.
One by one, splish splash splosh,
Phoebe counts her sheep!

At last poor Phoebe's quiet.
She doesn't make a peep.
Her eyes are closed, she's nodded off.
Phoebe is asleep!

"Result!" cheer Phoebe's naughty sheep.
Their night has just begun.
"We'd best be on our way," they say.
"It's time we had some FUN!"

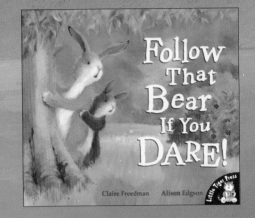

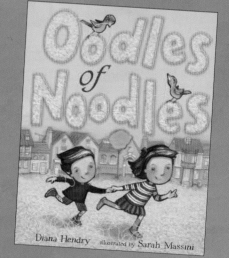
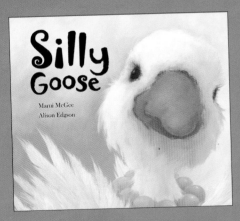